The Simple
Life of
MAX
the Dog

by
Vera
Thornton

The Simple Life of MAX the dog

Written and Illustrated by
Vera Thornton

in memory of my
Mom and Dad
Roy and Helen Thornton

and dedicated to
Morgan
Emily
and
Sophia

Vera Thornton
15251 Eddy Lk. Rd.
Fenton, MI 48430-1608
(810) 629-6144
web: www.verathornton.com

Published by Comet Publishing
U.S.A.
www.cometpublishing.com

Created and edited by David Kinder
Burton Printing Company/Comet Publishing
4270 S. Saginaw St.
Burton, MI 48529
(810) 742-3210
email: burtonprinting@sbcglobal.net
www.burtonprinting.com

Printed in Hong Kong
Library of Congress Cataloging-in-Publication Data on file.
ISBN: 978-0-9753741-3-9

Max didn't feel like other dogs. He didn't feel good about himself. He liked to run and play, but when it came to learning what other dogs knew, ...he was different. People couldn't carry him around, or dress him up in cute clothes. He didn't know how to hunt and fetch.

"Why can't I learn like other dogs?" Max thought. "Maybe I'm not smart! Maybe I'll never be smart! Maybe I just shouldn't even try!" Max lay on the sofa thinking. "What good am I anyway?"

One rainy, stormy day, when all the other dogs had gone home, or inside, Max lay on the couch watching the rain run down the driveway to the pasture and into the swamp on the other side of the road. When all of a sudden, he sat right up straight.

A car was crashed into the fence and Momma horse was running frantically in circles looking for her baby.

Max ran to the car. A man was getting out. He had a bump on his head and the fence was down. Max ran to the house barking as loud as he could. "What's wrong Max?" the farmer asked. Max barked even louder and ran toward the car with the farmer close behind.

Max ran to the mother horse and barked
and sniffed. Then he ran to the swamp.
There in the swamp, was the baby horse.
Her feet were stuck in the mud and the
grass was too slippery for her to climb out.

Max pulled on her halter. Then he went behind her
and nipped and barked and snaped at her tail.
"Go!" Max barked. "Go, Go!" Then he ran to
get the farmer.

The farmer threw a rope around the filly's neck and pulled. But it was no use, she was too tired! "Max," he said, "you have to nip at her when I pull! Make her try harder!"

Max nipped and barked and snapped at her tail. He didn't give up. The filly tried harder as Max nipped and barked.

At last she was free.

"Max"... the farmer said, "I always knew you were a great dog. You're the best!! Everyone has different talents and yours is being a herding dog. Not every dog is a herding dog, but you are!!"

"You may not do what other dogs do, but they can't do what you do either! Everyone is different and we each have to find our own talent. You sure found yours today!"

"Max... You Saved The Day!!"

Now that Max knew what his own talent was, he couldn't wait to practice. He wanted to be the best herding dog he could be. So he thought he would practice on something small first and work his way up to the big stuff. So bright and early the next morning, he went to the barn, where he found Mother hen with her chicks.

It took an hour and a half, but he finally got them where he wanted them. "Now that I've gotten better, I'll try something bigger," he thought....
"like geese!"

Now he was getting even better. "I have to practice, practice, practice!" He told himself and wanted to try something a little harder... "Sheep!"

Having moved the sheep to where he wanted them, he thought, "Maybe, it's now time to try COWS!"

The cows took longer because they lived down the road at the neighbor's farm. But he did it.

"Now, all there is left is horses!"

Horses would be his biggest test. If he could herd those horses, he would be the best Herding Dog he could be.

He Knew What
He Had To Do!!

now that Max knows what his talent is,
he just has to learn to slow down!
It's not going to happen all at once.

Max and his friends, (children from the neighborhood) were having a picnic in the back yard. They had been playing with some toy jewelry and Grandma had given each of them a dollar in change to spend later that day.

'Max Solves a Mystery"

Max was keeping a close eye on them, when Grandma came out and asked, "Why don't you children go check to see if the mail's here? And why are my clean clothes on the ground? And where are my clothes pins?"

"We Don't Know", someone said, "We didn't take them!" They all sang out happily. And off they ran down the driveway, with Max close behind.

They returned to find that something was different.
All of their mouths dropped open!
"My ring, it's gone!" "Gone" they all gasped "Maybe it's
on the ground!" They all checked the grass. But the
ring was no-where to be found. "And my beads,"
someone said, "They're gone too!"

Grandma came into the yard carrying ice cream. "After you eat your ice cream, please go get the eggs!" She asked. "And why are my clean clothes back on the ground?"

They ate their ice cream and talked about the mystery of the missing gems as they walked to the barn to gather the eggs. Max watched and listened. "Where did they go?" he thought. He would have to be quiet and watch. And think. "Things don't just fly away!" Max said to himself. So he laid quietly in the barn and watched through the door.

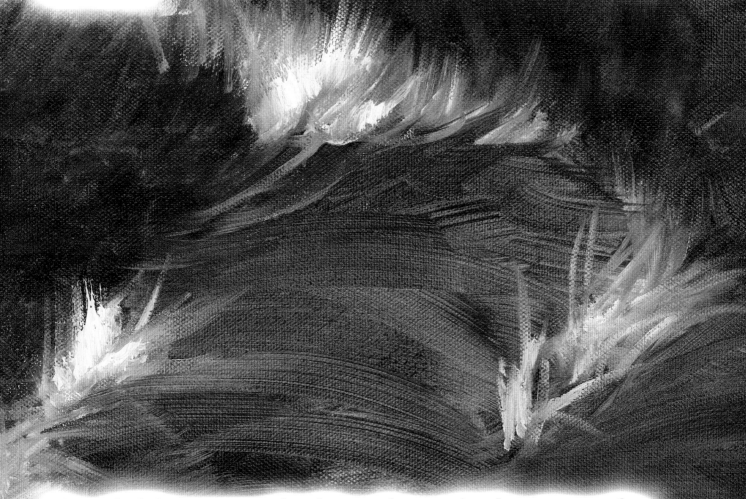

The children were looking through the straw for the eggs, when all of a sudden Max began to bark. He jumped to his feet and ran toward the back yard where...

There in the middle of the table was a crow, with a ring in his beak.

Max jumped and the crow flew. "Johnny!!" all the children yelled. Johnny the crow lived with a Native American neighbor on the other side of the river.

"Come on kids," Grandma said, "We're going to Johnny's house."

Johnny the crow nested in the barn. And there in the tool box were the missing items and a whole lot more. His owner explained to them that crows like to pick up anything shiny and will carry things away. (Even clothes pins)

The next day in the newspaper was an apology which read in part that, anyone missing shiny valuable items, may identify them and pick them up at Mr. Kinder's house.

The children all laughed when they talked about how Max solved the mystery and imagined Johnny the crow dressed in prison stripes and dragging a ball and chain. "Crime doesn't pay!" they laughed.

"Max"... Grandma laughed, "You solved that mystery by paying attention and listening. You watched and used your brain. Sometimes all we have to do is stay quiet and watch carefully! You're not just a herding dog, you're a detective!"